Son of Samson
and the Judge of God

The Judge of God

Requests for information should be addressed to:

Zondervan, *Grand Rapids, Michigan 49530*

Library of Congress Cataloging-in-Publication Data

Martin, Gary, 1956-
The judge of God / by Gary Martin; art by Sergio Cariello
p. cm. -- (The son of Samson; bk. 1)
ISBN-13: 978-0-310-71279-4 (pbk.)
ISBN-10: 0-310-71279-3 (pbk.)
1. Graphic novels. I. Cariello, Sergio. II. Title.
PN6727.M374J83 2007
741.5'973--dc22

2007003157

Series Editor: Bud Rogers
Managing Editor: Bruce Nuffer
Managing Art DIrector: Merit Alderink

Printed in the United States of America

07 08 09 10 11 12 • 10 9 8 7 6 5 4 3 2 1

Son of Samson and the Judge of God

series editor: bud rogers

story by gary martin

art by sergio cariello

ZONDERVAN®

CHAPTER 1
"GOD'S CHOSEN NAZIRITE"

IN THESE DAYS, ISRAEL HAD NO KING...

...AND EVERYONE DID WHAT WAS RIGHT IN THEIR OWN EYES.

SO THE LORD GAVE THEM INTO THE HANDS OF THE PHILISTINES!
IT'S THAT WHEY-FACED SIDON!
THEY'RE HERE TO PILFER OUR SUMMER HARVEST!
WE WON'T SURVIVE THE WINTER ON THE SCRAPS THEY'LL LEAVE BEHIND!

PARDON THE IGNORANCE OF A PASSING STRANGER...
...BUT WHY THE CLAMOR?

IT'S THE VILLAINOUS COMMANDER SIDON AND HIS SWAG-BELLIED SOLDIERS.
THEY'VE RETURNED TO LOOT THE TOWN'S MEAGER FOOD SUPPLIES!

THIS IS TROUBLESOME.
I WAS UNDER THE IMPRESSION THAT ZORAH HAD A REPUTATION OF HOSPITALITY.
OF ALL THE IMPERTINENT...

ALLOW ME TO HONOR YOUR PHILISTINE GUESTS...

...WITH A SERVING OF THIS FINE ZORAHIAN MELON.

GAUGING THE DISTANCE TO BE ABOUT 600 CUBITS*...
*OR 300 YARDS (A CUBIT WAS APPROXIMATELY 18 INCHES.)

...THE YOUNG STRANGER LAUNCHES THE MELON WITH THE FORCE OF A CATAPULT!

THESE HEBREWS FORGET THEIR PLACE.
I'LL NOT TOLERATE THEIR DEFIANT BLABBER. BEFORE WE FILL OUR BELLIES...
...GIVE THE TOWN LEADERS A GENEROUS SAMPLE OF THE PHILISTINE LASH!

HMM.
HEY, ARMAROS! IS THERE SOMETHING FALLING FROM THE HEAVENS, OR DID I HAVE TOO MUCH WINE LAST NIGHT?
I SEE IT TOO. AND BY DAGON, IT'S COMING RIGHT AT US!

KER-SPLAT!

THAP!

PLAP!
PHWAP!
THAP!

STAND YOUR GROUND, YOU CLAY-HEADED MISCREANTS!
RETREAT!
THE GOD OF ISRAEL RAINS WRATH UPON US!

LOOK! THEY FLEE LIKE BLUBBERING CHILDREN!
HAIL THE NEW GUARDIAN OF ZORAH!
HALLELUJAH!

BLESSED ANGEL WHO ADMINISTRATES GOD'S WRATH IN THE FORM OF PRODUCE, MAY WE KNOW YOUR NAME?

I ASSURE YOU; I'M NO ANGEL. MY NAME IS BRANAN. I SEEK MY GRANDFATHER, MANOAH.

ADONAI* BE PRAISED!
I'M MANOAH!
YOU MUST BE MY GRANDSON...
*HEBREW TERM FOR GOD, OR THE LORD.
...THE SON OF SAMSON!

DEAR ME! AFTER WATCHING YOU DEVOUR THAT MEAL...
...I WONDER IF IT WAS A MISTAKE TO CHASE AWAY THE PHILISTINES!

OOP!

AHH-HAHAHA!

NOT TO WORRY, MY BOY!
I'M WELL ACQUAINTED WITH HEARTY APPETITES. FEEDING YOUR FATHER WAS A FULL DAY'S WORK!

MY MOTHER, BACK IN GATH, SAYS FEEDING ME IS LIKE THROWING PEBBLES DOWN A BOTTOMLESS WELL.
I'M SURE SHE'S A REMARKABLE WOMAN. I WOULD BE HONORED TO MEET HER SOME DAY.
RAISING YOU ALONE, WHILE SAMSON GALLIVANTED AROUND THE COUNTRYSIDE, MUST HAVE BEEN A HEAVY YOKE.
MY POOR MOTHER ENDURED CONSTANT RIDICULE FROM HER PEOPLE, THE PHILISTINES, FOR INSTRUCTING ME IN THE LAWS OF GOD.
NOW THAT I'M EIGHTEEN, IT'S TIME I EASED HER BURDEN AND MADE MY OWN WAY. I WANT TO LEARN MORE ABOUT MY FATHER BY TRAVELING THROUGHOUT PALESTINE, RETRACING HIS RENOWNED FEATS.
ALONG THE WAY I HOPE TO DISCOVER GOD'S PURPOSE FOR ENDOWING ME WITH MY FATHER'S STRENGTH.

THEN LET US BEGIN YOUR JOURNEY WITH THE ASTONISHING TALE OF THE ANGELIC HERALD WHO FORETOLD YOUR FATHER'S BIRTH.
ONE DAY, THE ANGEL OF THE LORD APPEARED TO YOUR GRANDMOTHER, MY DEAR DEPARTED WIFE.
BEHOLD, YOU ARE BARREN AND HAVE NO CHILDREN. BUT YOU WILL BECOME PREGNANT, AND GIVE BIRTH TO A SON.
THEREFORE, DO NOT CONSUME WINE OR STRONG DRINK. AND DO NOT EAT ANYTHING THAT IS UNCLEAN.
AFTER YOUR SON IS BORN NO RAZOR SHALL TOUCH HIS HEAD, FOR HE WILL BE A NAZIRITE* FROM THE DAY OF HIS BIRTH.
AND HE WILL BEGIN TO DELIVER ISRAEL FROM THE HANDS OF THE PHILISTINES.
*A NAZIRITE TOOK A SPECIAL VOW TO DEDICATE HIMSELF TO GOD'S SERVICE. (TO LEARN MORE, READ THE BOOK OF NUMBERS, CHAPTER 6.)

"WHEN MY WIFE TOLD ME OF THIS WONDROUS MESSENGER, MY FAITH WAS WEAK. I NEEDED TO SEE HIM FOR MYSELF.
"GOD LISTENED TO MY PRAYERS, AND THE ANGEL OF THE LORD RETURNED AND REPEATED HIS INSTRUCTIONS.
"FOOLISHLY, I DID NOT REALIZE WHO HE WAS AND I INVITED HIM TO STAY AND EAT.
IF I STAY, I WILL NOT EAT YOUR FOOD...
...BUT IF YOU PREPARE AN OFFERING, OFFER IT TO THE LORD.
"SO I PLACED A YOUNG GOAT AND SOME GRAIN ON A ROCK TO BE A SACRIFICE TO THE LORD."

"MIRACULOUSLY, THE FIRE BLAZED UP FROM THE ALTAR, AND THE ANGEL ASCENDED FROM THE FLAMES TOWARD HEAVEN!"*
*READ THE ENTIRE ACCOUNT IN JUDGES 13.

THERE'S SOMETHING I CAN'T COMPREHEND. FROM THE ACCOUNTS I'VE HEARD, MY FATHER NEVER TOOK HIS NAZIRITE VOW SERIOUSLY.
IT SEEMS HIS ONLY ASPIRATION WAS TO GRATIFY EVERY WHIM OF HIS INSATIABLE HEART!
WHY WOULD ADONAI CHOOSE SUCH A FLAWED MAN TO DELIVER THE NATION OF ISRAEL?
THE QUESTION IS, MY DEAR BOY, WHY WOULD GOD CHOOSE TO DELIVER OUR UNREPENTANT NATION AT ALL?
FORTUNATELY FOR US, GOD IS MERCIFUL! AND DESPITE OUR FAILINGS, HE USES US TO ACCOMPLISH HIS DIVINE WILL. LIKE WITH YOUR FATHER...

"...EVEN THROUGH SAMSON'S *TRAGIC* AND HEROIC DEATH, GOD WAS ULTIMATELY *GLORIFIED!*"

THE FOLLOWING MORNING, BRANAN PACKS FOR HIS FIRST DESTINATION, RAMATH LEHI, THE PLACE SAMSON SLEW ONE THOUSAND PHILISTINES WITH A DONKEY'S JAWBONE.
RAMATH LEHI IS A DIFFICULT TWO-DAY TREK SOUTH FROM HERE.
TRY TO REACH THE YAFFA OASIS BY DUSK, SO YOU CAN REPLENISH YOUR WATER AND REST BEFORE YOU CONTINUE.
A WORD OF ADVICE: TRY NOT TO DRAW ATTENTION TO YOURSELF.
ALTHOUGH IT'S BEEN TEN YEARS SINCE THE DEATH OF YOUR FATHER ...
... HIS MEMORY IS STILL BITTER IN THE HEARTS OF THE PHILISTINE LORDS.

ONE LAST THING. YOUR NEW CAMEL, UZAL, HAS AN IRRITABLE DISPOSITION.
IT'S NOT WISE TO GET TOO CLOSE TO--
P-TEU!
HA HA HA
HA HA
NEVER MIND.
HA HA HA!

CHAPTER 2
"THE MELON OF DOOM!"

MIDDAY.
AS THE MERCILESS SUN BEATS DOWN ON BRANAN...

...HIS HEAVY EYELIDS SUCCUMB TO THE MONOTONY OF THE LONELY ROAD.

WHAT THE?!
NICE WORK, BRAN!
IN ONE IDLE-BRAINED MOVE, I'VE LOST MY RIDE AND MY WATER SUPPLY!
AND IT'S A FIVE-HOUR WALK TO THE OASIS!
MERCIFUL LORD! GRANT YOUR WITLESS SERVANT THE FORTITUDE TO CATCH THAT CANTANKEROUS FOUR-LEGGED SCOUNDREL!

THE YAFFA OASIS, FIVE HOURS LATER.

?

HHH

SPLASH
GULP!
GULP!
GULP!

GULP!
GULP!
GULP!

SQUIRT
GERRAUGH!
OH, HI, UZAL! FORGET SOMETHING BACK THERE?

ARE YOU THE OWNER OF THAT DETESTABLE BEAST?

UNFORTUNATELY.

THIS IS HOW THAT SURLY LOUT INTRODUCED HIMSELF!

HA HA! NO HARM DONE. WHAT'S YOUR NAME, LAD?
BRANAN.
I'M JOBAB. COME SHARE MY CAMPFIRE!

THANK YOU FOR YOUR GENEROUS HOSPITALITY!
I'M TRAVELING TO RAMATH LEHI. DO YOU KNOW HOW FAR IT IS?

IT'S THREE OR FOUR LEAGUES* DUE SOUTH. ALTHOUGH, I COUNSEL YOU TO AVOID THAT PLACE.
*ONE LEAGUE IS APPROXIMATELY THREE MILES.

THE RESIDENTS OF THAT VILLAGE ARE EXCEEDINGLY ODD. A LEGENDARY FEAT OCCURRED THERE FIFTEEN YEARS AGO.

"THE MIGHTY SAMSON HAD SLAIN SCORES OF WRETCHED PHILISTINES AND WAS RESTING IN A CAVE.
"THE MEN OF JUDAH WERE AFRAID OF PHILISTINE REPRISALS, SO THEY CAME TO NEGOTIATE HIS CAPTURE."
WHAT HAVE YOU DONE? DON'T YOU KNOW THE PHILISTINES RULE OVER US?
AS THEY DID TO ME, I HAVE DONE TO THEM!
WE'VE COME TO TIE YOU UP AND HAND YOU TO THE PHILISTINES.
SWEAR TO ME THAT YOU WILL NOT KILL ME YOURSELVES.

"THE MEN AGREED AND BOUND SAMSON WITH TWO NEW ROPES...
"...AND LED HIM TO THE PHILISTINES.

"WHEN THE PHILISTINES SAW SAMSON APPROACHING...
"...THEY CAME AT HIM, SHOUTING WITH FURY!

"THE SPIRIT OF THE LORD CAME UPON SAMSON MIGHTILY, AND HE SNAPPED THE ROPES LIKE BURNT THREAD!

"AS THE ENRAGED PHILISTINES CHARGED, SAMSON LOOKED AROUND FOR A WEAPON...
"...AND FOUND A DONKEY'S JAWBONE.

"ON THAT DAY THE GREAT AND MIGHTY SAMSON STRUCK DOWN ONE THOUSAND PHILISTINES!

"THEN SAMSON PRAYED TO GOD TO QUENCH HIS MASSIVE THIRST.
"GOD OPENED THE GROUND, AND WATER GUSHED FORTH.
"SAMSON NAMED THE SPRING EN HAKKORE.*
*SPRING OF THE CALLER. (TO READ ABOUT THIS STORY, SEE JUDGES 15.)

TODAY, RAMATH LEHI HAS BECOME THE PLACE OF AN ECCENTRIC CULT.
WHY ARE YOU GOING THERE?
SAMSON WAS MY FATHER!
WELL, PRAISE ADONAI! I'M HONORED TO SHARE MY CAMP WITH THE SON OF--

CAPTAIN! WE'LL BED DOWN HERE FOR THE NIGHT.
RECRUIT VOLUNTEERS FROM THESE HEBREWS TO SET UP MY TENT. THEN THE MEN CAN CONFISCATE WHATEVER PROVISIONS THEY CAN FIND.

THE PHILISTINE SOLDIERS RANSACK THE OASIS CAMPSITES...

...GREEDILY PILFERING WHATEVER STRIKES THEIR FANCY.

I'M NOT GOING TO SIT BY AND--
HOLD, YOUNG ONE!

IT'S NOT WISE TO REVEAL YOUR IDENTITY TO THE PHILISTINES, AND ESPECIALLY TO COMMANDER SIDON.
HE HAS A DARK HEART, WHICH CAN ONLY BE HEALED BY GOD.

LATER THAT NIGHT.

MAYBE A FLOCK OF BIRDS DROPPED THE MELONS ON US.
ARMAROS, YOU'RE FULL OF CAMEL PIE! IT'S A QUESTION OF WEIGHT RATIOS...

KLONK!

MEANWHILE, INSIDE COMMANDER SIDON'S TENT...
THESE BAUBLES ARE THE ONLY VALUABLES THE MEN COULD SCRAPE UP.
BAH! THIS RUBBISH WILL ONLY FETCH A FEW SHEKELS.

THUMP
KRASH!
CAPTAIN?

CAPTAIN! ANSWER ME!

WHA--?

THWAK!
UHH!

BY DAGON, THESE HEBREW SCUM WILL...
...HUH?

AAAH!

MOMENTS LATER.
YOU MAGGOT-FACED PUSTULES! I'LL SKEWER YOUR CARCASSES!
OH, MY! YOU KISS YOUR MOTHER WITH THAT VENOMOUS MOUTH?

HOLD THIS.
AND I'D ADVISE YOU NOT TO LET GO.
YOUR COMMANDER SEEMS TO LACK A LENIENT NATURE.
AND SO, BRANAN AND HIS FELLOW TRAVELERS BID FAREWELL TO THEIR NEW PLAYMATES.

CHAPTER 3
"CULT OF RAMATH"

UZAL, DO ME A FAVOR. TRY NOT TO OFFEND THE LOCALS.
I DON'T WANT ANY TROUBLE HERE.

SALUTATIONS TO YOU, STRANGER.

THAT'S A FINE-LOOKING ANIMAL YOU HAVE THERE!
DELBER? ISN'T THAT A FINE-LOOKING ANIMAL?
FINE-LOOKING!

I AM EZER, KING OF SHEBA. I NEED LIVESTOCK FOR MY ROYAL CARAVAN.

WILL YOU TAKE THREE SHINY RED RUBIES FOR HIM?

UMM?

WATERS! I COMMAND THEE TO PART!
KER-SPLASH!

DON'T BOTHER ABOUT HIM. HE'S SIMPLE-MINDED. HE THINKS HE'S MOSES!
SO, WE HAVE A DEAL THEN. AGREED?

IT'S A TEMPTING AND GENEROUS OFFER...
...BUT I'LL HAVE TO DECLINE.
I COULD NEVER SELL UZAL. WE HAVE A BOND TOO WONDROUS FOR WORDS!
?!

I WOULD LIKE TO PROPOSE A COUNTER OFFER. MY PROVISIONS ARE LOW. MAY I PURCHASE SOME FOOD?
FORTUNE SMILES UPON YOU, STRANGER. WE HAVE THE FINEST UNLEAVENED BREAD IN THE LAND!
THE PRICE IS ONE RED RUBY.

HOLD ON!
HEY YOU CHILDREN! GET DOWN FROM THERE!

?

HERE YOU ARE...
...ONE SHINY RUBY!
HEE-HEE!

ENJOY!

BEHOLD! THE CAMEL BLASPHEMES EN HAKKORE!
IT IS FORBIDDEN TO DRINK FROM THE SACRED SPRING!
UZAL! COME AWAY FROM THERE!
PLEASE FORGIVE THIS LUMPISH BEAST. HIS MANNERS ARE SADLY DEFICIENT.

I APOLOGIZE FOR THE TRANSGRESSION. PLEASE TELL ME OF ANY OTHER EDICTS I SHOULD KNOW ABOUT.
IT IS UNLAWFUL TO TRANSPORT LIZARDS IN YOUR PANTS ON THE SABBATH.
AND CODFISH!
FOREMOST, OUTSIDERS ARE FORBIDDEN TO ENTER THE TEMPLE OF THE SACRED JAWBONE.

IS THIS THE VERY JAWBONE SAMSON USED AGAINST THE PHILISTINES?
OF COURSE.
BUT WHAT ABOUT YOUR BREAD?

I'M NOT THAT HUNGRY. IT'S ALL YOURS!
UNHAND IT, BEETLE BREATH!
IT'S MINE, YOU PAUNCHY FLAP DRAGON!

WHO DARES!?
JOLT HEAD!
CANKER FACE!
ALARM!
AN OUTSIDER DESECRATES THE SACRED TEMPLE!

IN AWE, BRANAN APPROACHES AN ALTAR THAT HOLDS THE WEAPON OF HIS FATHER.
BLASPHEMER!
THE OUTSIDER MOCKS THE HOLY ALTAR!
SLAY THE INFIDEL!

IN A TWIST OF IRONY, BRANAN WIELDS THE JAWBONE AGAINST THE BERSERK ATTACK.

DO MY EYES DECEIVE?
ARRROO!
WHA--?
ARROOO!

BEHOLD, FAITHFUL ONES!
OUR LONG AWAITED DAY IS UPON US!
I PROCLAIM THE GLORIOUS RETURN OF... THE MIGHTY SAMSON!

HAIL SAMSON!
HAIL SAMSON!

OH, GREAT ONE, FORGIVE YOUR WRETCHED SERVANTS FOR THEIR IDIOCY!

I PROFUSELY APOLOGIZE FOR NOT RECOGNIZING YOU SOONER.
FRANKLY, WE WERE EXPECTING YOU TO BE A BIT...
...OLDER.

BUT REST ASSURED, SAMSON THE MAGNIFICENT, WE HAVE DILIGENTLY PREPARED FOR YOUR WONDROUS RETURN!

LET US IMMEDIATELY PROCEED TO THE HALLOWED DWELLING OF THE MAIDS IN WAITING!
ONE MINOR POINT. I'M NOT...
SNIFF! SNIFF!

UMM!

THIS IS A DAY OF JUBILEE! OUR MAIDENS' FIFTEEN-YEAR VIGIL CAN NOW BE REWARDED WITH MARRIAGE TO THE ALMIGHTY SAMSON!

YOU CALL THIS AN AMPLE SERVING? THIS PORTION COULDN'T NOURISH A FLEA!

MORE MUTTON! AND THIS TIME, IT BETTER BE HOT!
THESE DATES ARE A DISGRACE! THROW THEM OUT AND GET ME FRESH ONES!

SECONDS LATER.

THE FOLLOWING DAY, IN THE BUSTLING CITY OF HEBRON.
UZAL, I'M SO FAMISHED, I COULD EAT A CAMEL!
NO OFFENSE.

GREETINGS STRANGER. BY THE LOOKS OF YOUR WORN-OUT SANDALS, YOU HAVE TRAVELED MANY LEAGUES.
I SAY YOU DESERVE A NEW PAIR!
ASK ANYONE IN HEBRON. MY SELECTION IS UNSURPASSED!
IF I HAD MONEY, I WOULD FEED MY STOMACH BEFORE I SHOD MY FEET.
YOU'RE A STRAPPING YOUNG MAN. YOU COULD COMPETE IN THE GAZA GATE FESTIVAL AND WIN A SUBSTANTIAL AWARD.
EVERY YEAR DURING THIS TIME, THE FESTIVAL COMMEMORATES...

"...WHEN THE MIGHTY SAMSON CARRIED THE GATE OF GAZA THIRTEEN LEAGUES* TO THE OUTSKIRTS OF HEBRON!"
*APPROXIMATELY THIRTY-EIGHT MILES

CHAPTER 4
"GATES OF GLORY"
THE CONTESTANT WHO CARRIES HIS GATE THE FARTHEST WINS THE PRIZE OF THIRTEEN SHEKELS!*
REPRESENTING THE THIRTEEN LEAGUES TO GAZA!
*EQUIVALENT TO ABOUT TWO MONTHS' WAGES

READY... COMMENCE!
HUMPH!
HMMM.

ERRRIP!

THE PHOENICIAN IS LOOKING STRONG!
BUT WHAT'S THIS!? A LATE CONTENDER IS MAKING A MOVE!
WE HAVE A NEW CHAMPION!
INTERESTING.

THAT NIGHT, WHILE BRANAN CELEBRATES HIS VICTORY...

...SEVERAL LEAGUES FROM HEBRON, THE BROODING SIDON RECEIVES A VISITOR.
ZIBEAL TO SEE YOU, COMMANDER.
FORGIVE THE INTRUSION, YOUR EMINENCE, BUT I HAVE VITAL INFORMATION YOU'LL FIND OF GREAT INTEREST!

EASILY WORTH THE PALTRY SUM OF... FIVE SHEKELS?

MAKE YOUR REPORT, CUR! I'LL DECIDE IF YOU DESERVE A REWARD.

IN HEBRON TODAY, A YOUNG MAN WITH THE BRAWN OF SAMSON HEFTED THE GATE OF GAZA WITH REMARKABLE EASE.
WHAT RELEVANCE IS THIS TO ME?

IT'S OBVIOUS HE'S RESPONSIBLE FOR INFLICTING YOUR HUMILIATION AT THE YAFFA OASIS THAT LORD PATHRUS WILL HOPEFULLY NEVER HEAR OF.

I'D ADVISE YOU TO HOLD YOUR MOCKING TONGUE, OR I'LL HAVE IT REMOVED!

DRAG THIS FOBBING JACKAL OUT OF MY SIGHT!

THEN ASSEMBLE THE MEN.
WE'RE MARCHING TO HEBRON!

THE NEXT MORNING BRANAN RESUMES HIS JOURNEY AND, BY CHANCE, GLANCES BACK AT HEBRON.
BILLOWING SMOKE? I WAS THERE NOT AN HOUR AGO!

FLAMES HAVE CONSUMED THE VINEYARDS! HOW COULD THIS HAPPEN?

LISTEN WELL, HEBREWS. FOR AS YOU CAN SEE, I'M IN NO MOOD FOR TRIFLES!
I WANT THE WHEREABOUTS OF THE YOUNG GATE CARRIER, OR I'LL SET A TORCH TO YOUR TOWN!

THIS IS MY FAULT! I ENTERED THAT CONTEST FOR PERSONAL GLORY.
NOW OTHERS ARE SUFFERING BECAUSE OF MY FOOLISH PRIDE!

MERCIFUL FATHER...

...I BEG YOUR FORGIVENESS, FOR I AM A SINFUL MAN.
GRANT ME YOUR MIGHTY SPRIT FOR WHAT I'M ABOUT TO DO!

SIDON! WHAT'S THAT DISGUSTING ODOR?
DON'T TELL ME...

...YOU SOILED YOURSELF WHEN I HAULED YOU UP THAT TREE?

CLEVER WORDS FROM A WALKING CORPSE.
SEIZE THE WHELP!

BLA-DOW!

THWAP!
THWAP!
THWAP!

KER-SKRUNCH!

LET'S TEACH THAT SIDON SCUM SOME HEBRON JUSTICE!
PLUNK!
PLUNK!
THUMP!

GLORY TO THE ALMIGHTY BRANAN!
HAIL OUR CHAMPION!

GIVE THE GLORY TO GOD, AND PRAISE HIS NAME!

A FEW DAYS LATER, IN THE PHILISTINE CITY OF ASHKELON.
COMMANDER SIDON?

LORD PATHRUS WILL RECEIVE YOU NOW.

THIS WAY, COMMANDER.
HEH-HEH!

LORD PATHRUS, IT'S GOOD OF YOU TO...
SPARE ME THE PLEASANTRIES, COMMANDER!
I KNOW OF YOUR FAILURE TO CAPTURE THE YOUNG HEBREW OUTLAW!

MY LORD, I ASSURE YOU...

YOUR ASSURANCES ARE OF LITTLE COMFORT CONSIDERING YOUR SEVERE INCOMPETENCE!

ANOTHER ISRAELI HERO OUR PEOPLE WILL NOT TOLERATE.
NEED I REMIND YOU HOW MUCH WE SUFFERED AT THE HANDS OF SAMSON?
I WANT THIS RUFFIAN APPREHENDED IMMEDIATELY!

YOU KNOW MY RECORD OF LOYAL SERVICE. I'M UP TO THE TASK!

NO NEED. I'VE ALREADY OBTAINED THE AID OF THE ONE WHO CONQUERED ISRAEL'S LAST HERO.
YOU'RE TO INVESTIGATE A DISTURBANCE AT THE MARKETPLACE.

THAT IS, IF YOU CAN HANDLE A FEW DISGRUNTLED FISH MERCHANTS!

YOU HAVE MY LEAVE.

JAVAN! BRING IN MY GUEST.

WELCOME! MY HUMBLE ABODE IS HONORED BY THE PRESENCE OF THE ILLUSTRIOUS--
DELILAH!
CONTINUED IN THE SON OF SAMSON, BOOK 2: "THE DAUGHTER OF DAGON"

CRAZY HADAD'S SANDAL WORLD
TRADE IN YOUR OLD PAIR FOR A 10% DISCOUNT!
LOCATED IN CENTRAL HEBRON (ACROSS FROM BASKETS-R-US).
OPEN SIX DAYS A WEEK (CLOSED ON THE SABBATH).
WORK SANDALS
MADE FROM TOUGH OX-HIDE!

WE HAVE THE LARGEST SELECTION IN EASTERN JUDAH!
YOU WANT IT, WE HAVE IT!
SPORT SANDALS
LIGHTWEIGHT FOR RUNNING FASTER AND JUMPING HIGHER!
DRESS SANDALS
CRAFTED FROM RICH CORINTHIAN LEATHER!
LADIES SANDALS
ALL THE LATEST PHILISTINE STYLES!
AT CRAZY HADAD'S, MY PRICES ARE SO LOW, YOU'LL THINK I'M CRAZY!

"THE ADVENTURES OF YOUNG BRANAN"
ONE DAY, ON THE OUTSKIRTS OF THE PHILISTINE TOWN OF GATH...

I'M NOT TALKING JUST TO HEAR MY HEAD ROAR. I SAID NO!
BUT FATHER, WHY NOT?
THE LION WE'RE HUNTING IS A MAN-KILLER! THAT'S WHY YOU CAN'T COME WITH US. NOW GO BACK TO TOWN!
AWWW!

HE ALWAYS TREATS ME LIKE A BABY!
WE NEVER HAVE NO FUN!

WELL, LOOKIE-LOOKIE! IT'S THAT BEEF-WITTED BRANAN!
DANG! HE'S CARRYING THOSE WATERBAGS LIKE THEY WAS NOTHIN'!
I COULD DO THAT IF I WANTED!

I THINK HE'S *CREEPY!*
MY FATHER SAYS *BRANAN* AND HIS *MOTHER* DON'T WORSHIP OUR GOD, *DAGON.*

THEY PRAY TO A WEIRD *HEBREW* GOD THAT HAS *NO* NAME.

COME ON. *LET'S* TEACH HIM A *LESSON!*

HEY, BRANAN! THOSE LOOK MIGHTY HEAVY. IT WOULD BE A PITY IF YOU SPILLED THEM.
WHY DON'T YOU GET YOUR FATHER TO HELP YOU?

OH, I FORGOT. YOU DON'T *HAVE* A *FATHER!*
AH HA HA!

IF I WERE YOU...
OOF!

HAW HAW! STU-PID BRA-NAN!

HEE HEE!
QUICK! HIDE IN THE CAVE!

YOU SEE HIM?
NO.

HEY, ZED. WHY WE HIDING? IT'S THREE AGAINST ONE!
BECAUSE, THAT BOY'S AN OX!

ONE TIME, BRANAN'S *MOTHER* HURT HER *FOOT* WHILE WORKING IN THE FIELDS.
THAT BOY *LIFTED* HER OFF THE GROUND AND *CARRIED* HER LIKE A WOUNDED BIRD *ALL* THE WAY HOME!

WITH HIS BRAWN, I DON'T WANT HIM GETTIN' HIS PAWS ON ME!
HEY! I'VE NEVER BEEN IN HERE. LET'S SEE HOW FAR IT GOES.

I BET MARAUDERS HIDE TREASURE IN HERE!

I DON'T LIKE THIS. I CAN'T SEE A THING!
JORY, DON'T BE SO MILK LIVERED!

I DON'T CARE. I'M GOING BACK!
ME TOO!

WAIT! I JUST TOUCHED SOMETHING STRANGE.

IT MIGHT BE BANDIT PLUNDER!

AAAAAHHH!

OUT OF MY WAY, JORY! YOU'RE SLOWER THAN DONKEY SPIT!

BY DAGON, MOVE YOUR TAIL!

WHEN WE GET HOME, I'M TELLING YOUR MOTHER YOU SWORE AT ME!

ROARRRR!!!

GERRRRR!

HE'S *BLOCKING* THE ENTRANCE! *WE'RE TRAPPED!*

GER-ROARR!

GERR...

?

THA-THOOM!

RUN, BRANAN!

LATER, BRANAN RETURNS TO TOWN TO AN UNEXPECTED CELEBRATION.
PRAISE ALMIGHTY DAGON!
HURRAH!

PARDON ME, SIR? WHY THE CLAMOR?
OUR PHILISTINE LORDS CAPTURED THE OUTLAW HEBREW LEADER!

THE MENACING BRUTE SLEW MANY OF OUR PEOPLE.
NOW HE'S A BLINDED, WHEAT-GRINDING BUFFOON! HA!

BRANAN ENTERS HIS HOME AND FINDS HIS MOTHER IN TEARS.
MOTHER?

WHY DO YOU WEEP?

OH, BRANAN!
SINCE THE DAY OF YOUR BIRTH I'VE KEPT SOMETHING FROM YOU.

PROMISE ME YOU WON'T REVEAL THIS SECRET TO ANYONE, OR THE PHILISTINE LORDS WILL COME AND TAKE YOU AWAY!
I PROMISE.
IT'S TIME I TELL YOU WHO YOUR FATHER IS...
THE END

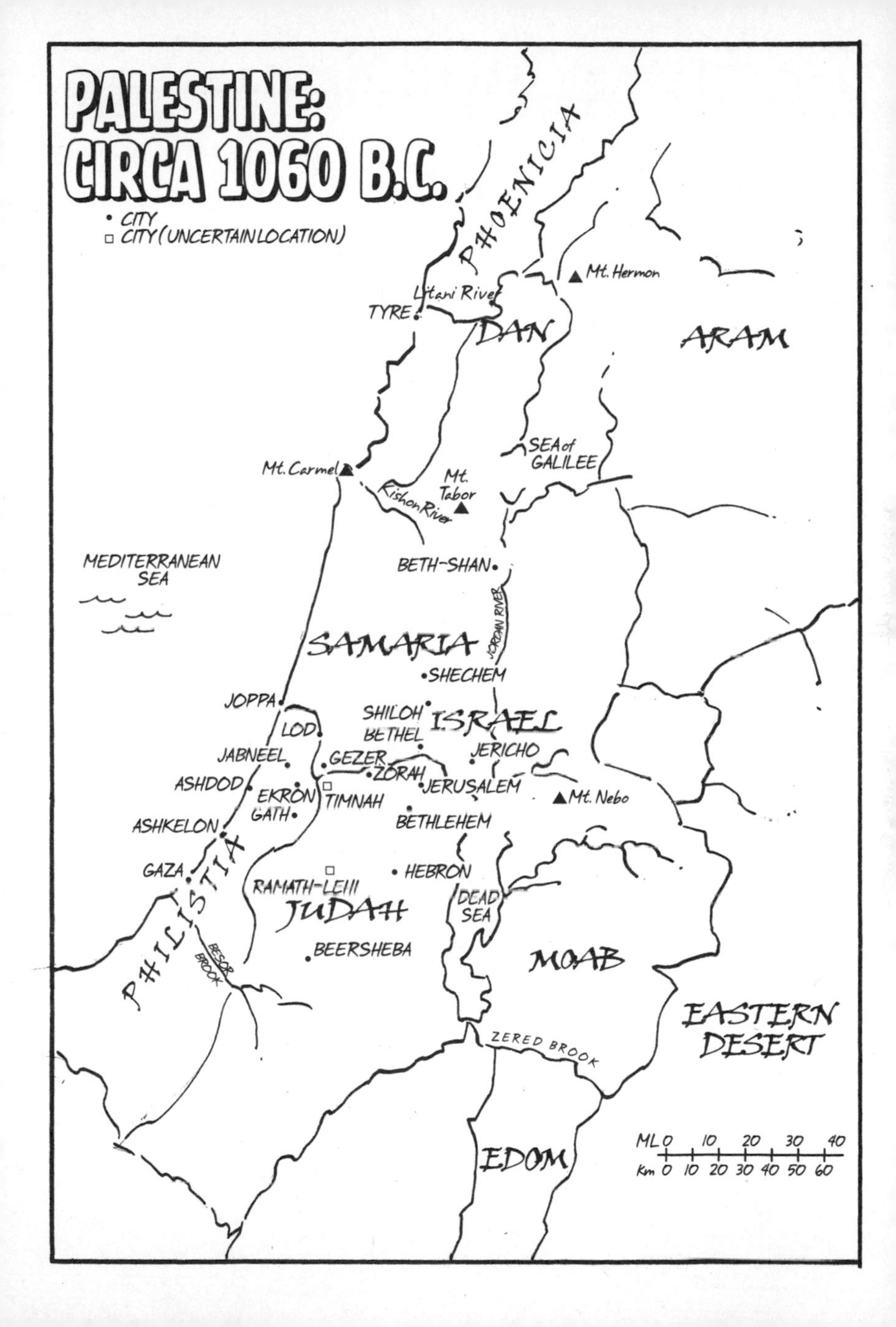
PALESTINE: CIRCA 1060 B.C.
• CITY
□ CITY (UNCERTAIN LOCATION)
PHOENICIA
Mt. Hermon
Litani River
TYRE
DAN
ARAM
SEA of GALILEE
Mt. Carmel
Mt. Tabor
Kishon River
MEDITERRANEAN SEA
BETH-SHAN
JORDAN RIVER
SAMARIA
SHECHEM
JOPPA
SHILOH
ISRAEL
LOD
BETHEL
JABNEEL
GEZER
JERICHO
ZORAH
ASHDOD
EKRON
TIMNAH
JERUSALEM
Mt. Nebo
GATH
BETHLEHEM
ASHKELON
PHILISTIA
GAZA
HEBRON
RAMATH-LEHI
DEAD SEA
JUDAH
BEERSHEBA
BESOR BROOK
MOAB
EASTERN DESERT
ZERED BROOK
EDOM
ML 0 10 20 30 40
Km 0 10 20 30 40 50 60

LIFE IN THE TIME OF SAMSON
VOW OF THE NAZIRITE

LIFE IN THE TIME OF SAMSON

THE PHILISTINES

KNOWN AS THE "PEOPLE OF THE SEA," THE PHILISTINES ARE BELIEVED TO HAVE MIGRATED TO PALESTINE FROM THE ISLAND OF CRETE. COMPARED TO THE ISRAELITES, THE SOPHISTICATED PHILISTINES WERE AN ADVANCED CULTURE OF ARTISANS, CRAFTSMEN, AND ARCHITECTS. HAVING THE ABILITY TO FORGE IRON WEAPONS (WHICH THE HEBREWS DID NOT YET POSSESS) GAVE THE PHILISTINES AN ADVANTAGE IN BATTLE. THEY DOMINATED THE NATION OF ISRAEL FOR FORTY YEARS UNTIL ISRAEL REPENTED, AND (WITH GOD'S HELP) DROVE THE PHILISTINES FROM THEIR LAND AND RECLAIMED THE CITIES THE PHILISTINES HAD TAKEN. (READ 1 SAMUEL 7 FOR THE STORY OF ISRAEL'S DELIVERANCE FROM THE PHILISTINES.)

Branan
STANDING SIX FEET TWO INCHES AND WEIGHING TWO HUNDRED FORTY POUNDS, THE EIGHTEEN-YEAR OLD SON OF SAMSON INHERITED HIS FATHER'S INCREDIBLE STRENGTH. RAISED BY HIS PHILISTINE MOTHER, BRANAN NOW TRAVELS THE ANCIENT LANDS OF PALESTINE, RETRACING THE LEGENDARY DEEDS OF THE FATHER HE NEVER KNEW.
06

Manoah
FATHER OF SAMSON AND GRANDFATHER OF BRANAN, MANOAH RESIDES IN THE CITY OF ZORAH. THE ONLY KNOWN RELATIVE TO BRANAN'S FATHER, MANOAH IS AN IMPORTANT CONNECTION TO BRANAN'S HERITAGE. (TO LEARN MORE ABOUT MANOAH, READ JUDGES 13-14:9.)

Sidon
A COMMANDER IN THE PHILISTINE ARMY, THE FORTY-YEAR-OLD SIDON IS A VETERAN OF NUMEROUS MILITARY CAMPAIGNS. WITH A LEAN SIX-FOOT FRAME, SIDON IS FORMIDABLE IN BATTLE AND A MASTER OF DIVERSE WEAPONRY. HIS CONTEMPT FOR THE ISRAELITES IS A PRODUCT OF HIS DARK AND BITTER HEART.
06

SAMSON WAS GREATLY EMPOWERED BY GOD WITH AWESOME STRENGTH, YET HE FAILED TO FULLY UTILIZE HIS EXTRAORDINARY GIFTS FOR GOD'S GLORY. SAMSON WAS A JUDGE OF ISRAEL FOR TWENTY YEARS. THE SON OF SAMSON UNDERTAKES HIS JOURNEY OF DISCOVERY (APPROXIMATELY) TEN YEARS AFTER SAMSON'S HEROIC DEATH. (THE EXPLOITS OF SAMSON ARE CHRONICLED IN THE BOOK OF JUDGES, CHAPTERS 13-16.)
SAMSON

Young Branan
WITH THE INHERITED MIGHT OF HIS FATHER BUDDING IN HIM, EIGHT-YEAR-OLD BRANAN IS LARGE FOR HIS AGE. GROWING UP WITHOUT A FATHER HAS MADE HIS LIFE DIFFICULT. AND BECAUSE BRANAN AND HIS MOTHER LIVE IN THE TOWN OF GATH AMONGST THE PHILISTINES, THEY ENDURE MUCH RIDICULE FOR WORSHIPING THE GOD OF ISRAEL.

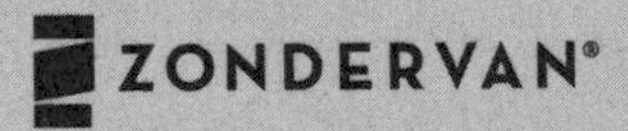

We want to hear from you. Please send your comments about this book to us in care of zreview@zondervan.com. Thank you.

Grand Rapids, MI 49530
www.zonderkidz.com

ZONDERVAN.com/
AUTHORTRACKER
follow your favorite authors